Night of the Pumpkinheads

written by
MICHAEL J. ROSEN

pumpkin carvings by
HUGH MCMAHON

DIAL BOOKS FOR YOUNG READERS • an imprint of Penguin Group (USA) Inc.

O ne muggy October, a patch of pumpkins grew plump and restless.

"We've sat here *for weeks* with nothing to do," complained Jackpot, head of the Union of Pumpkinheads.

"Yeah! And soon, we'll be plunked on some porch with a stupid grin on our faces," added Jackie-Oh.

"For once, why can't *we* dress up and go out? Those kids think their costumes are *sooooo* spooky!" Jackpot mocked.

Instantly, ideas of creepy, chilling costumes filled the air above the patch like the fireflies.

"Ooooh, I got it! I'll be a cootie! Kids hate cooties—no, wait, I'll be a cat! A *mean* one! The *Scaredy*-Cat!"
"I'll go as a saber-toothed tiger!"

"Or a cobra!" shouted Jackie-Oh.

"Okay!" Jackpot shouted. "Let's have a contest for the scariest pumpkinhead! Whoever *really* spooks the kids will be crowned head of our *own* holiday: Jack-o-Ween!"

The patch of Jacks cheered.

"Start dreaming up your ideas," said Jackpot. "I'll be the judge!"

The colossal Jacks figured it was only natural to go as the Earth's first giants.

"What's scarier than prehistoric beasts scarfing down people like animal crackers?" laughed Jack of Spades.

"I call mastodon!"

"Brontosaurus!"

"I'm triceratops!"

"You guys be the *veggie* dinos," JackKnife said. "*I'm* a carnivore: T. rex! I can already hear those kids running for mommy!"

Outside the old shed, several white pumpkins voted to be ghosts.

"Naw, they're too friendly!" other Jacks argued.

Finally JackRabbit suggested a mime. "They're even creepier than mummies!"

By nightfall, the white pumpkinheads had formed a teetering, towering zombie mime!

"Hey? Hey! What about us?" A chorus of turnips
poked out of the soil. "Can we be in the contest?"
  Rows of radishes, rutabagas, parsnips, and leeks all echoed, "Yeah!"
  "No way!" the pumpkinheads all answered. "This is *our* holiday."
  "Honestly," Jackpot laughed. "How on earth could you, you little tubers
and roots, reign over Jack-o-Ween?"

Meanwhile, at the miniature-pumpkins' meeting, the Jacks worried that no one would notice them, let alone find them spooky. But then those small pumpkinheads found some *big* ideas:

"We'll be cannibals!"
"No . . . icky eyeballs!"
Finally, itty-bitty Stonewall
Jackson said, "Let's be . . . *bees!*
Swarms of killer bees!"

On the hay wagon, odd green pumpkinheads carefully balanced on one another, imitating Frankenstein's creature. Other Jacks fashioned a wavy Lock Ness Monster with slithery, seaweed-tangled humps.

"Oooh! We're . . . *sickening!*" Jacques Cousteau beamed.

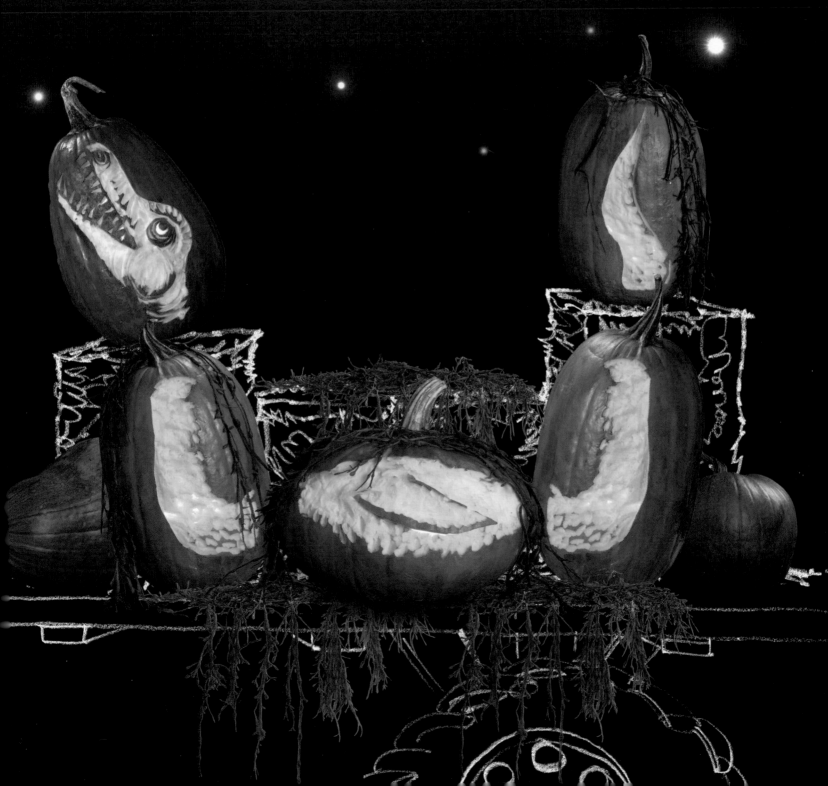

Halloween night, the pumpkinheads resembled the entire neighborhood's nightmares, all assembled at the garden gate. "So . . . gargantuan spiders from outer space." Jackpot reviewed the contestants. "Nice! A skeleton . . . blood-thirsty bat-heads . . . ooh! and a slithering, gooey blob of Jacks—The Slime! Perfect. I believe we're ready to roll!" Jackpot announced.

Trailing slippery pumpkin guts and seeds, The Slime heaved onto the first porch the Jacks encountered. The kids just snickered and tossed them lollipops.

"They weren't even a *little* scared," admitted Jackaranda as they slid down toward the sidewalk.

"Nice try," Jackpot offered. "Maybe that house has especially brave kids . . . ?"

Next, killer bees swarmed trick-or-treaters at a street corner. "Everybody *buzz!*" whispered Little Jackal.

"Hey, do you guys have any bubble gum?" a Tooth Fairy asked. "I'll trade you for anything in my bag."

"But—but we're killer bees!" buzzed Cracker Jack. "We're deadly!"

A gorilla replied, "Any of you want licorice? I hate it . . ."

One by one, Frankenstein's monster, the skeleton, the zombie mime—all the Jacks tried to spook the trick-or-treaters. But the kids just giggled. No one seemed even slightly frightened. And now it was time for the kids to head home and the pumpkinheads to return to the patch.

"Jacks . . . we did our best," said Jackpot. "Next year, with more time, we—"

Just then, a shrieking crowd charged
down the street, spilling candy, losing wigs,
stumbling over capes and monster feet.

"They're after us!" a Spider-Man shrieked.

"Disgusting!" a mermaid screamed. "They're
gross! Keep away!"

"Mommeeeeee, help!"

Jackpot shouted, "What's going on?
What's frightened them?"

"It's . . . it's the *vegetables!*"
the Jacks chorused.
    Dressed in nothing but their leafy
tops, the left-behind garden veggies
shuffled down the emptied street.
The pumpkinheads all groaned.
    "Okay," Jackpot reluctantly
admitted. "You win. You plain veggies
scared the kids more than us
dressed-up pumpkinheads. You can
reign over Jack-o-Ween—"

"You mean, *Bean*-o-Ween!" the crowd of vegetables cheered.

Turning toward their patch, Jackpot grumbled, "Those veggies—they . . . they hiJACKed our holiday!"

How to Carve Your Own

Caution: Carving requires using sharp knives carefully and with some force; ask an adult to do the actual carving.

1) At your local pumpkin patch, choose a round, medium-size pumpkin. Give it a quick wipe with a damp cloth or sponge.

2) Ask an adult to carve a hole in the bottom. You reach in and scoop out the seeds and goop. (Save the seeds! See the recipe for Roasted Pumpkin Seeds). To make the carving easier, carefully shave off some of the interior pumpkin flesh with an ice-cream scoop.

3) With a washable marker, draw your own scaredy-cat on one side of the pumpkin. Use the whole face of the pumpkin for the cat's features.

7) Carve out the ears and then stand them upright in front of their holes. Use toothpicks to secure the ears if necessary.

8) Ask an adult to use a smaller knife—like an X-Acto knife—to make shallower cuts (these don't go all the way through the pumpkin) to create the nose, whisker dots, and tufts of fur.

9) With a damp sponge or paper towel, wipe off whatever remains of your original drawing. To make your carving last longer, rub all the cuts with petroleum jelly or spray with lemon juice.

Scaredy-Cat Pumpkin!

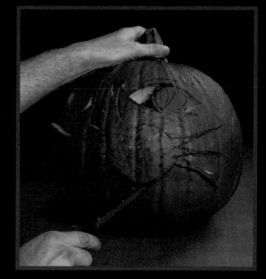

4) Here's Hugh McMahon's drawing just for inspiration. Draw the ears on each side; they will be completely cut out and stood up on each side of the face. (See step 7.)

5) Time for the carving! Have an adult carve out the eye holes with a long knife—like a fruit and vegetable knife—working slowly and carefully.

6) Now, with the same knife, slice through the outer outline of the muzzle, chin, and whiskers so that you can slide them out together in a single piece. Pull the shape out just a bit and let it rest in place.

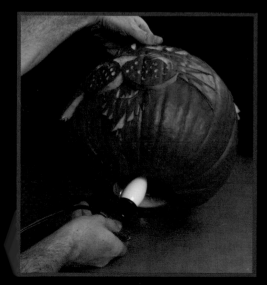

Roasted Pumpkin Seeds Recipe

10) Have an adult insert a small lightbulb into the hole at the base of your pumpkin. A candle will create a dimmer glow. (Be sure you don't leave the pumpkin lit if someone's not in the room.)

11) Light up your scaredy-cat jack-o'-lantern! (To make it last longer, keep it in a cool, dark place when it's not lit. If it starts shriveling, refresh it in a bucket of cold water.) Meow!

* * * * * * * *

Rinse the seeds, pick off the stringy bits of goop, and spread the seeds on a baking sheet misted with vegetable-oil spray. Lightly salt them, and have an adult pop them in a 325° F oven for 20 minutes or until toasty, stirring them to toast the other side after 10 minutes. Let them cool—**delicious!**

* * * * * * * * *

For Jennie, the pumpkin queen
—MJR

To my parents, Franklin and Irene McMahon, for
supporting my pumpkin carving as a profession
—HM

DIAL BOOKS FOR YOUNG READERS
A division of Penguin Young Readers Group • Published by The Penguin Group
Penguin Group (USA) Inc., 375 Hudson Street, New York, NY 10014, U.S.A.
Penguin Group (Canada), 90 Eglinton Avenue East, Suite 700, Toronto, Ontario, Canada M4P 2Y3 (a division of Pearson Penguin Canada Inc.)
Penguin Books Ltd, 80 Strand, London WC2R ORL, England • Penguin Ireland, 25 St. Stephen's Green, Dublin 2, Ireland (a division of Penguin
Books Ltd) • Penguin Group (Australia), 250 Camberwell Road, Camberwell, Victoria 3124, Australia (a division of Pearson Australia Group
Pty Ltd) • Penguin Books India Pvt Ltd, 11 Community Centre, Panchsheel Park, New Delhi - 110 017, India • Penguin Group (NZ), 67 Apollo Drive,
Rosedale, North Shore 0632, New Zealand (a division of Pearson New Zealand Ltd) • Penguin Books (South Africa) (Pty) Ltd, 24 Sturdee
Avenue, Rosebank, Johannesburg 2196, South Africa • Penguin Books Ltd, Registered Offices: 80 Strand, London WC2R ORL, England

Text copyright © 2011 by Michael J. Rosen
Pumpkin sculptures, vegetable sculptures, and illustrations copyright © 2011 by Hugh McMahon
Photography copyright © 2011 by William Brinson
All rights reserved

Designed by Jennifer Kelly
Text set in Birdlegs

Manufactured in China on acid-free paper

Library of Congress Cataloging-in-Publication Data
Rosen, Michael J., date.
Night of the pumpkinheads / written by Michael J. Rosen;
pumpkin carvings by Hugh McMahon.   p. cm.
Summary: Determined to make Halloween a frightening
night of the pumpkinheads, the pumpkins transform
themselves into a variety of scary monsters and then
head for town hoping to terrify everyone they meet.
ISBN 978-0-8037-3452-4 (hardcover)
[1. Halloween—Fiction. 2. Pumpkin—Fiction.
3. Vegetables—Fiction.] I. McMahon, Hugh, ill. II. Title.
PZ7.R71868 Ni 2011   [E]—dc22
2010039314

10 9 8 7 6 5 4 3 2 1

The art for this book was created by digitally
assembling photographs of Hugh McMahon's
pumpkin carvings and pencil drawings.